D0915764

PILGRIM AT SEA

Drawings by Emil Antonucci

Vintage Books
A Division of Random House
New York

PILGRIM AT SEA
Pär Lagerkvist

TRANSLATED FROM THE SWEDISH BY

NAOMI WALFORD

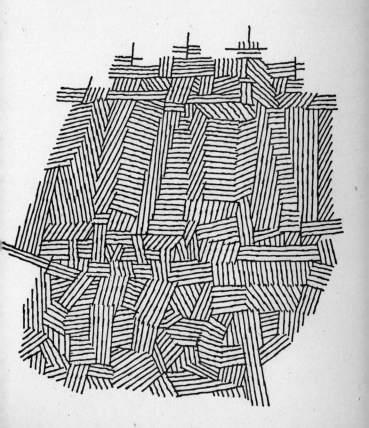

First Vintage Books Edition, March 1982

*Copyright © 1964, by Random House, Inc. and
Chatto & Windus, Ltd.*

*All rights reserved under International and Pan-American
Copyright Conventions. Published in the United States by
Random House, Inc., New York. Originally published in
Swedish as Pilgrim pa havet. © 1962, by Pär Lagerkvist and
in English by Random House, Inc., New York, 1964.*

Library of Congress Cataloging in Publication Data

Lagerkvist, Pär, 1891-1974.

Pilgrim at sea.

Translation of: Pilgrim pa havet.

Originally published: New York: Random House, 1964.

I. Title.

[PT9875.L2P5413 1982]   839.7'372   81-16076

ISBN: 394-70821-0   AACR2

Manufactured in the United States of America

PILGRIM AT SEA

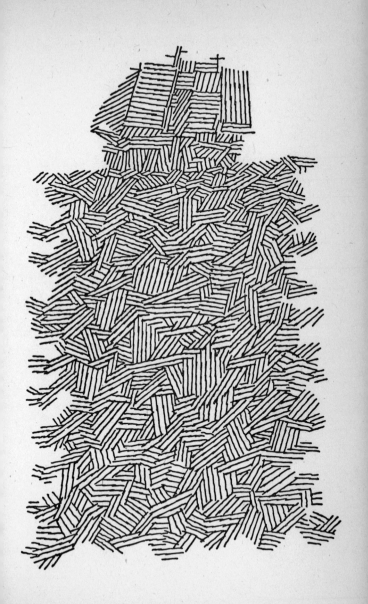

WHEN THE PILGRIM had boarded the pirate ship that was to carry him to the Holy Land he found rest, and was no longer troubled by any kind of dread. A peace such as he had never known descended upon him as he lay on his bunk in the bowels of the ship, his hands clasped upon his often uneasy breast. Wind and sea raged outside; he knew that the vessel was a miserable old hulk and the crew a feckless rabble, yet he felt strangely secure; he surrendered himself utterly to them and to the turbulent elements. He had paid his passage; he had given the men all he possessed—all his ill-gotten money—and they had furtively counted it, caring nothing for the blood upon it. Now he and they were out upon the tossing seas, bound for the land to which they had promised to take him. He believed this; for some reason he felt more confident than ever before in his life. Although he remembered their roar of laughter as they shoved off from the quay he was unconcerned, and doubted not that they would carry him to that distant, longed-for land.

Soon he fell asleep, as if lulled by the seas—by the ocean itself that surrounded him with its restlessness and uncertainty and yet brought him peace.

When he awoke it was no longer so dark, and he saw that a man was sitting there, looking at him. He seemed to have been doing so for some time, as if waiting for him to wake, and observing him as he slept. He was a brutal-looking fellow with a big face and wide mouth, beardless but with thick, somewhat grizzled hair and dense, dark eyebrows that enhanced the hardness and keen scrutiny of his gaze.

"Are you awake now?" he asked, in a voice that one might have expected to be rougher and more hostile. "Then perhaps you'll tell me who you are and what you're after. What's your business aboard?"

"You know that. You must know where this ship is bound for."

The man muttered something inaudible.

"Yes. Of course," he said then, drily.

For a time he surveyed the newcomer, scanning his thin, hard face and the long hairy hands that lay clasped upon his breast.

"You don't look like a pilgrim," he remarked.

The other gave him a quick, almost anxious glance; then cautiously, as if hoping the movement would pass unnoticed, he unclasped his hands.

"You look like the rest of us, and that's good. I think it's a good thing for you. Though of course you're fair-skinned and light-haired. Where are you from?"

There was no reply.

"And you're not dressed like one, either. Like a pilgrim, I mean. Why not? What's your name?"

Still no reply.

"You're thinking it's none of my business," said the man with a little laugh. "And you're right. All the same, you might tell me."

"Tobias."

"I see. Well, it makes no difference what one's

called or where one comes from, once one's aboard this ship. Nothing matters any more then."

He continued to look at him with a piercing, searching gaze that made Tobias feel uncomfortable.

"I suppose you meant to sail in the regular pilgrim-ship, didn't you?"

"Why, of course."

"And you missed her. Was that it?"

"Yes."

"I thought I'd heard so. And then you had to take this one instead. And she'll do, too. Though it's not a very usual way to travel to the Holy Land," he added, laughing. "Still, if the skipper promised to take you there, then he will, of course. Sure to. He's an honest man—no question of that. And you've paid, so it's all settled. Did you give him all you had?"

"Yes."

The man stroked his mouth as if to hide a smile.

"He must have thought you wouldn't need any money from now on. That's about it, and of course he's right. Better for him to have it. Safer. That's what he thought.

"If by chance you have any left," he went on, "don't let it be seen. Hide it . . . You might need it when you reach that Holy Land—if you do reach it. And of course you will. Sure to. But tell me, why do you want to go there?"

"Why?"

"Yes. I'd like to know. I'd like you to tell me about it."

"Surely that's my affair."

"Of course it is. That's why I'd like you to tell me. What makes you so keen? For you are, you know. Keen enough to pay any sum—all you possess. Odd, don't you think?"

Tobias made no answer.

"The regular pilgrim-ship has sailed—the one carrying the true pilgrims, I mean—so you rush down to the harbour and take passage in any old boat, in any old weather. Curious, surely!"

Again Tobias made no answer.

"Not that this isn't a good ship—a very good ship—I don't mean that. I've been aboard her now for many a long year, so I ought to know. And she carries a good crew: decent, honest fellows. I can vouch for that. You're safe with them: they can weather any storm. Not the timid sort—they're afraid of nothing. They fear nothing, neither god nor devil. So if anyone could take you to the Holy

Land, we could. But tell me, why are you so anxious to get there?"

Tobias still made no reply, and the other remained silent too, scanning that hard, stubborn face that was too tense, as if bolted and barred.

"I've seen many of the real pilgrims," he continued after a while. "One runs into them down in the harbour as they wait for their ship to sail. I usually have a chat with them and ask them questions, though I don't know why. I don't like them. Indeed I don't. They revolt me. When you've looked at their faces for a while it's good to get to sea again. Especially when it blows as it did last night. I wonder how they fared: it would be amusing to know.

"No, I don't like them. I don't like you either. But you don't look like them. You don't look like a real pilgrim."

Once again Tobias gave him an uneasy glance which the other appeared not to notice.

"What hairy hands you have! Ferrante has hands like that, though his hairs are black. Watch out for him. He's the only one you need beware of; the rest are decent fellows—the lot of them—as I said. The only one you must watch is the one with hairy hands like yours. Easy enough to remember."

He paused, but continued to observe Tobias as narrowly as before.

"It's your own affair. So you say. And that's why you're not with the ordinary lot, the ordinary flock of sheep that trail along behind that cross, possessing a soul in common, as it were. You come alone. You make pilgrimage on your own, in your own way. You probably haven't even got a cross—or have you? Not so much as a rosary with a little cross on it. No, I saw at once that you hadn't—you had nothing in your hands—they were empty. No, a cross wouldn't suit hands like those—like Ferrante's.

"Yet you want to be a pilgrim—you want to get to the Holy Land. What's the point? What business has a man like you there?

"If you're so set on it, of course we'll take you. That goes without saying. We'll do it somehow or other, just as the skipper promised. When we pledge our word we keep it—we're like that. And you've paid. You've handed over all you possess, like a true Christian. Though you don't look like one: you look like an honest man. Like the rest of us. You'll fit in well here, you'll see; you'll become just like us, as soon as you've got used to one or two things that may surprise you at first. And with those hands you can certainly pull your weight: they look used to any job—the sort of job that may turn up here, too. I believe you've come aboard the right ship.

"Have you ever been to sea before?"

"No. Never."

"So you know nothing about it?"

"Nothing."

"Then you've a lot to learn. One learns a great deal from the sea. I tell you, you may walk through country after country, through lands and through huge cities you've never seen before, and over the whole wide earth, and never learn as much as you will from the sea. The sea knows more than anything else on earth if you can get it to teach you. It knows all the ancient secrets, because it's so old itself —older than all things. It knows your own secrets too, make no mistake. If you give yourself to it entirely and let it take charge—not jib or dig your toes in about trifles, not expect it to hear your petty murmurings while it is speaking, while it's hurling itself over the ship—then it can bring peace to your soul. If you have one. And if peace is what you want. I don't know about that, and it's none of my business. But be sure, you'll win no rest for your soul except from the sea, which itself never finds rest. That's how it is. That I can tell you.

"No, there's nothing like the sea. No such friend, no one who can so help and save a poor devil. This is what I wanted to tell you. And you can rely on what I tell you and be sure that it's true. I know what I'm talking about.

"Though perhaps I ought not to call it my friend —that may be presumptuous. I ought to speak about it with more humility and veneration—with greater reverence. As of something holy. For that's what I feel. The sea is the only thing I do feel is holy. And every day I give thanks that it exists. However it may storm and rage I thank it. Because it gives peace. Not security but peace. Because it's cruel and hard and ruthless, and yet gives peace.

"What should you do in the Holy Land when there's the sea—the holy sea?"

He sat plunged in his thoughts and seemed no longer aware of the other man's presence. His head was sunk on his breast, and on that big face was a look of introspection and mournful pondering.

"When I first came aboard this ship," he went on after a time, "I'd never seen the sea before. Much else had I seen—too much. I'd seen people—too much of people. But never the sea. Therefore I'd never understood anything—never grasped anything at all. How can one grasp anything of life—understand and penetrate men and their lives—until one has learnt from the sea? How can one see through their empty strivings and odd ambitions until one has looked out over the sea, which is boundless and sufficient in itself? Until one has learnt to think like the sea and not like these restless creatures who fancy that they're going somewhere, and that this going is the most important thing of all—that the goal is the meaning and purpose of their life. Until one has learnt to be carried along by the sea, to surrender to it utterly, and cease fretting about right and wrong, sin and guilt, truth and falsehood, good and evil—about salvation and grace and eternal damnation—about devil and god and their stupid disputes. Until one has become as indifferent and free as the sea and will let oneself be carried, aimless, out into the unknown—surrender utterly to the unknown—to uncertainty as the only certainty, the only really dependable thing when all's said and done. Until one has learnt all that.

"Yes, the sea can teach you much. It can make you

wise, if that's what you want to be. It can teach you to live."

He fell silent, and Tobias lay looking at him, wondering greatly at what he had said. Curious too about the man himself: who he might be to talk in this way, with that heavy, coarse face—coarsened perhaps by the sea, which he called holy. The holy sea . . . whatever he might mean by that. Hard to say. But he remembered the strange peace that had fallen upon himself, there in darkness and storm when he surrendered to them—when he went to rest with the sea. Without fear, without a care for anything.

Not to trouble oneself so; to find peace . . . Not security, but peace.

Not to chase so eagerly after some goal—some purpose—as he had done; not to inflame and drive oneself on towards one particular object. Not to keep on judging oneself, blaming oneself for one's misdeeds, for one's falseness and dishonesty; for being perhaps no true pilgrim, and for the blood that might be on the money that pays for one's passage to the Holy Land . . . that is, if there *is* a holy land, and not just the sea . . .

Not to worry so much, not to be so distraught and

despairing because one has attained no certainty and is sure of nothing—nothing at all . . . To be content with uncertainty, content and happy with it; to choose it. To choose unknowing and uncertainty . . . To choose oneself as one is. To dare to be what one is, without self-reproach.

And to choose the sea, the undependable, boundless, unknown sea, and an endless voyage without any fixed goal—without any goal at all . . .

Thus he thought as he looked at the man who had caused him so to think; the man who sat beside him and no longer seemed to notice him and who spoke no further to him, and whose gaze, which before had been so penetrating and searching, now seemed quite disengaged from anything about him: absent, remote. Was he looking out over his beloved sea, or over something to which he gave that name? His stern, weather-beaten face no longer seemed so grim; it had grown a little gentler, almost soft. Tobias could discern it more clearly now, for the light had grown stronger.

After a while the man awoke from his thoughts and looked at him, smiling a little in embarrassment at having been so abstracted.

"You'll come up on deck now, won't you?" he said. "Surely you don't mean to lie there all day!"

Tobias rose, and together they climbed the dim ladder leading to the deck.

Full sunlight, bright sunlight flooded the wide ocean and there was not a cloud in all the sky. The expanse of waters seemed endless and land was nowhere in sight. The sea still ran high, though it had dropped a little during the night, and here and there spray whirled from the waves. The wind blew fresh and the vessel was scudding under full canvas straight out to sea. So far no reefs had been taken in, but the men were standing by in case of need—in case anything should happen on this hazardous voyage. But the ship seemed to be handling herself; she rode the seas well and seemed built for just such weather as this. The men did not look at the newcomers, though of course they noticed them, and they gave no greeting. At the helm stood a huge fellow with arms and legs like sledge-hammers; everything about him was massive and oversized; his head alone was quite small and completely hairless, with two thick rolls of flesh at the back of his neck. He looked like an ogre, yet there was a good-humoured smile on his great thick lips. Again and again he glanced astern, on his guard against the heaviest of the seas.

Beside him stood a slouching, shabby figure, squat and punily built, with a slack, sour face and piercing little eyes. He threw a rapid and seemingly indifferent glance at Tobias, and then turned his back upon him. Tobias recognised him as the man who had counted his money the evening before, and realised that he was the skipper. This surprised him somewhat.

Seas burst continuously over the deck, sending water surging back and forth across it. Tobias had difficulty in keeping his feet; he staggered, and looked for something to hold onto. Next to him a man was standing, jeering at him. He was tall and gangling, the same height as himself and just as lean and sinewy, but his hair hung in a black fringe over his forehead and there was a dark stubble of beard on his morose, unfriendly face. His mouth was thin and pinched, and altogether he had a re-pellent appearance. Now and again he glanced at the skipper, and once when the latter nodded to him he hauled on the starboard sheet with his long, thin, black-haired hands, which clutched the line like claws.

The man who had accompanied Tobias up on deck had gone to attend to his duties, leaving Tobias alone with this distasteful-looking character. To avoid him, Tobias moved over to the port side of the ship. Here stood a man who seemed almost to welcome him; at least he was willing to talk. The wind in the sails and the continuous hum of the rigging made it difficult for them to hear each other, but the fellow moved close up against him and began warily trying to elicit from him what manner of man he was. Failing in this—for Tobias made no response—he confined himself to glancing at him sideways. He was a weedy little fellow with sloping shoulders and hollow chest; his face was narrow and pointed and quite colourless and his neck as skinny as that of a plucked bird. His eyes were small and shifty, ingratiating; he seemed anxious to please, and to behave as the other would wish him to do.

Tobias easily persuaded him to tell him something of the other men on board: the sour-faced, shabby fellow beside the giant was indeed the captain of the ship, and the one they all feared; the giant possessed brute strength and nothing more, but was a useful man in need, and the tall sinewy one was called Ferrante: a good comrade and the best seaman aboard. His own name was Giusto and he was really not much of a seaman; he attended to other matters, he said with a smirk on his grey, ratlike face, and stroked his mouth.

Tobias was curious above all to know who the strange man was who had visited him below in the fo'c'sle, who watched him as he slept and afterwards talked to him so strangely about things which perhaps Tobias, too, had borne in his heart, but which he had never thought that a man might dare to say, or even think. The man who had uttered words that might come to mean much to him—liberate him perhaps, and make him free.

Giusto was more than willing to talk about this man, and leered in advance at what he was going to say. Glancing in his direction he lowered his voice, though in such a wind it was quite unnecessary, and spoke under his sour breath right into Tobias' ear.

That fellow was an unfrocked priest—though who would have guessed it? No one could have believed that such a rascal had once been a servant of god. Yet it was said that when he first came, his head was shaven and he was terribly thin and pale —quite different from the man he was now. Giusto had never seen him thus, nor had any of the others, for it was long ago, a very long time ago; he was the senior aboard—senior to everybody else, including the skipper. Perhaps he had been with the ship as long as she had existed. Giusto couldn't tell.

How old was he? Hard to say. He looked like an old salt, all right. Such fellows were said to be so tanned and seasoned as to have no particular age. He was not much of a seaman—he just fancied he was—although he liked the sea; well, he must like it, since he had followed it for so long. "And it may be just as well that he's no longer ashore—no longer a priest, I mean—for so godless a man I've never met in all my life."

Tobias must have looked surprised and perhaps even incredulous, for Giusto went into a long explanation of just how godless this ex-priest was— how abominable a blasphemer and lecher—the worst that could be. At last he put his hand to his little rat's mouth and with a snicker told how at one of their ports of call he had a whore whom he called "the daughter of god" because she was of the same people as our saviour. Whenever they put in there he lay with her, saying that she too could bring salvation and that it was probably god's will, although she was the worst drab one could find in any port. And if that was not to be a blasphemer and whoremonger at one and the same time, then what was? And if satan were not satisfied with such a sinner, what *did* he want? Eh? "I believe he'll burn in hell-fire so long as there's a crumb of fuel left. Don't you?

"But it's a funny thing," he went on without a pause. "He's such a kind fellow—kind and friendly to everybody. He's always been kind and good to me, so I shouldn't say a word against him, or tell you any of this. He's the same to everyone, and everyone likes him; it's only Ferrante who doesn't think much of him—and the skipper, of course, who likes nobody. He's a terrible sinner, no question of that—but a *good* man, and that's the truth.

"His name? You don't know it? I thought you did. It's Giovanni. He's called Giovanni, after the disciple *he* loved most, remember? Giovanni. Yes, that's his name, however he came by it. But a fellow's got to be called something, I suppose."

Tobias cast a shy, wondering glance at the man

they were speaking of: the big man who had come to him down there in the half-dark and opened up a new world, as it were, a new life for him, and who was now busy with something in the bows—averted, faceless—with his broad, powerful back turned towards him.

Tobias moved away a little from the talkative man with the sour breath, and when he was once more by himself he pondered what he had heard.

Giovanni . . . the disciple whom *he* loved best . . .

Land was sighted ahead—a little piece of land, a small island that rose above the horizon and drew gradually closer. The hills upon it became clearer; at first they looked bare and bleak, but later one saw that their slopes were clad with small grey trees, no doubt olives, with vineyards between them. Along the narrow shoreline, now more clearly discernible, grew tall trees and spreading, luxuriant greenery of all kinds. The soil there was evidently fertile: the most fertile of all the island. As they approached, a fragrance such as Tobias had never known wafted towards them. Mighty stone pines grew upon this shore, lifting their crests against the clear sky, and other trees unknown to him soared on even mightier trunks from the fruitful soil, wreathed with myrtle and ivy or other climbing plants, as if the earth in its prodigality would have all things grow and thrive.

At one point along the coastline there was an unexpected inlet, a small opening leading into a perfectly circular lagoon, which offered the best and safest harbour imaginable, completely protected from any ocean swell. They steered through the narrow entrance, riding the turbulent waters there with practised skill, and found themselves in that calm pool where scarcely a ripple stirred.

In fact, this peaceful haven was the crater of an extinct volcano. The whole island was igneous and completely undermined; and was dotted all over with hot springs, sulphur-pools and places where steam rose continuously from the ground. Yet all was bathed in fragrance and clothed in the rich loveliness and prodigality of nature.

At the further side a big, handsome ship was moored, with her stern to the quay and a sturdy anchor hawser running down from her bows. All her sails had been lowered and were drying in the sun, so that the tall rigging was bare. The deck was crowded, not with seamen but with people of every sort, both men and women, wandering about with nothing to do. This was the pilgrim-ship for which Tobias had come too late.

They glided in and lay to beside her.

Giovanni, who was standing in the bows, slung their hawser ashore to a shabby-looking fellow whom he seemed to know well, and then glanced contemptuously at the captain of the pilgrim-ship, who was leaning over the rail in evident anxiety lest the newcomer should scrape the side of his fine vessel. This lay very high in the water and their own craft looked puny and pitiful beside her: battered and ill-kept, with patched and dirty sails. Some of the crew of the handsome ship came to look down at the other for a while, making some pitying comments. The idle pilgrims also gathered at the rail, for variety's sake, and loitered there.

Giovanni glared at them all in fury.

"What are you doing here? Scared to put to sea because it's blowing a bit? You weaklings—you cringing curs! Running for port just because there's a little sea on—and in that great ship of yours! Are you going to stay here in this puddle, then, with your damn fancy boat? Weren't you supposed to be going to the Holy Land? Well, weren't you? To his tomb—to the places where he was tortured and where he died? And you scurry into this puddle because you think it's blowing a little outside. You miserable bastards, seeking shelter on your way to Golgotha! Did *he* do that—did they let him? But you're doing it. And do you imagine he'll welcome you and be glad and grateful to you for coming to greet him in his own country and to see the kind of life he lived when he was a man like you, and was saving you, being crucified for your sake? That's what you think, isn't it? You think he'll be overjoyed to see you, and his father delighted to receive you some day into the kingdom of his glory—you who were so kind as to visit all the places where his son suffered and died. What will he say, do you suppose, when he receives such eminent guests? Shall I tell you? Shall I? Pay attention, then! Listen!

"'You cowards!' he'll say. 'You damned cowards! How do you expect to enter my kingdom if you run for port on the way? Do you think I'm going to let you in? Do you imagine I want gutless creatures like you? You must know that I want *men*— not a cowering herd.'

"Damn it, look at your faces! Makes one sick to

see them. He'll be sick, too. He'll spit in your eye when you try to get into his kingdom, and tell you to go to hell instead. That's what he'll do, be sure of that!"

They were all listening in amazement to this violent outburst, which was delivered in a tremendous voice so that those above him might hear it, and with passionate vehemence, despite the seemingly jesting words.

Not only those who were the targets of his ire listened to him with astonishment, but the people on the quay as well. These seemed to consist chiefly of loafers from the town and other yet shadier characters, and they all laughed loudly, greatly appreciating this free entertainment. The pilgrims, however, merely gaped, too stunned even to resent his derision and his appalling blasphemies. For a time Giovanni continued his impassioned outcry without stopping, pouring forth his hatred and contempt for them and their ship and all that was implied by the very existence of such riff-raff and its sanctioned voyaging upon the sea.

Meanwhile, as everyone's attention was diverted by this, a curious activity had developed in the bows of the newly-arrived vessel. Mysterious bundles and bales were being hastily passed ashore into the hands of certain ruffians, who vanished with them into one of the narrow alleys leading away from the dock. Little Giusto was superintending, with the help of the giant and Ferrante. The big man showed himself to be not only strong but unexpectedly agile and swift in his movements, despite his enormous size; while Ferrante, quite unconcerned, attended to his part of the task with a sombre, scornful demeanour towards everything and everyone about him, including Giovanni and his oration. They were both strong men and they worked quickly, but always under the vigilant supervision of the little ratface.

No one noticed their actions, not even the prying excisemen, who were doubled up with laughter like all the rest, and had eyes and ears only for Giovanni and his flow of eloquence. When all was done, all cleared, and Giusto had reported to the skipper, the latter moved stolidly forward and entered upon a lengthy argument with a fat man on the quay, until at last the fat man paid up what was due. The skipper seemed to feel no gratitude for Giusto's efficient services; at least he showed none, and his face wore its customary look of discontent.

At last the pilgrims reacted to all the mockery and

disgrace, contempt and derision to which they and their enterprise had been exposed; and they did so in an unexpected and rather strange manner. They neither defended themselves nor retaliated. They merely lifted their voices in their pilgrim-song: a song not composed by them, but lovely in itself and beautifully sung. Its theme was the heavenly Jerusalem, the city for which they yearned and for which they were bound. All listened to it with respect and in deep silence; even the roughs on the quay were reverent, and the excisemen. All stood with their faces upturned to the singers, listening. Giusto too listened, with his little rat's face raised in reverence, craning his neck with its big Adam's apple; there was real emotion in his incessantly blinking little eyes. The skipper alone, with a shrug, turned his back on it all, and Ferrante's contemptuous face remained unchanged.

Certainly a marvellous power dwelt in those people, though almost all of them must have been worthless—perhaps even despicable. They held their indifferent audience—the riff-raff on the quay—in awestruck silence, utterly transformed, if only for a little while. A remarkable power indeed, from wherever it came.

Tobias looked up and listened like the rest, but somewhat apart. He was very grave and his gaze was fixed upon the singers. It would have been hard to guess his thoughts, for his face, as usual, revealed nothing, although it was less stubbornly reserved than usual. His mouth was half-open, like a child's, and his lips moved a little as if he wanted to sing too, but didn't know the words.

He had not joined in the general laughter at Giovanni's outburst. This may have been because he was not a jocular man by nature, or because of something else—something more. One trait of his distinguished him from the great majority: he was constantly engrossed—perhaps even obsessed—with essentials, and with nothing else. From his rugged, mask-like face one could see that he was denied many human joys and perhaps was freed from many petty cares. It would have been no more than just if this were true.

He was unaware that Giovanni was close behind him—that he had come and taken his stand there—until he heard his petulant, scornful voice:

"There's your pilgrim-ship that you wanted so much to sail in! Why don't you board her?"

Tobias turned in distress and looked into that

embittered, agitated face. He hardly recognised it. Was this really the man who had spoken those memorable words to him, below, in the bowels of the ship?

He knew it was. And beneath the mockery and wrath—mere incidentals—he perceived his true face, heavy and serious, marked by long and anguished reflection. That face was dear to him. He would not be parted from it.

He did not answer the question; and Giovanni's eyes took on a triumphant, almost wicked glint on perceiving that this odd pilgrim had chosen not the handsome pilgrim-ship but their own dirty, battered old hulk, of which one might expect anything rather than a convenient passage to the Holy Land. Clearly he did not wish to arrive there in the manner of those others.

Now, after this brief but profitable visit, his companions cast off and set sail once more. What little wind entered the harbour was against them, so that they had to tack out and it was some time before they drew away to any distance from the other vessel.

"Greetings to the Holy Land, if ever you dare to go there!" shouted Giovanni from the stern. "And to the son of god—if he has a son!" he added, with a coarse laugh that sounded strangely false, coming from him.

When they had passed out through the narrows and the wind filled their sails once more, they all burst into a roar of laughter at their successful coup. Even Ferrante laughed, and Giovanni uttered a rumbling, good-humoured guffaw. The giant's laughter was phenomenal: his jaws opened in a huge red cavern that might have engulfed anything. Compared with it, Giusto's mirth was no more than a joyous little squeak from that pointed muzzle of his. The skipper held his hand before his mouth and looked down in embarrassment; no one could tell whether he was really laughing or not.

Tobias stood in the bows, not sharing in the general exultant merriment which he barely understood and to which he was indifferent. He looked out over the sea before him, landless, boundless, infinite. The wind had dropped somewhat, yet it still blew freshly about him. The waters were calmer, too; they no longer ran white, but moved in a long swell over which the ship glided softly and swiftly, with almost imperceptible motion, carefree and proud, indifferent to all but herself, under the patched sails which, however dirty, were filled with the fresh breeze.

Whither were they bound?

He did not know. Did any of them? When they resumed their course after leaving the safe harbour behind them they seemed merely to set it according to the wind and the vessel's best point of sailing. So at least it seemed to him as he looked ahead over the endless waste of waters, over this sea that opened out boundlessly on all sides as if it knew no limits . . . as if the sea alone existed . . .

The holy sea . . .

No fixed goal, no goal at all . . .

Only the sea . . . The holy sea . . .

They sighted a stranded three-master on the starboard bow; she was cast up on a reef and lay on her beam-ends. She must have struck during the raging gale of the night before, and become a total wreck. The spot was notorious for its danger, for here lay tiny, uninhabited islands surrounded by treacherous, hidden rocks, and this was not the first vessel that had foundered among them.

They altered course and headed for the wreck.

Probably she had been abandoned by her crew, whether or not they had survived. There seemed little likelihood of their having escaped; yet as the distance diminished it could be seen that there were people aboard. A few, at any rate. They made urgent signals, and as the vessel approached they gesticulated in great joy.

The rescuers put about and lay to beside the wreck, while the castaways watched the skilful manoeuvre and greeted them eagerly. They threw down a ladder and the skipper climbed aboard the wreck, followed by Ferrante, the giant and little Giusto. Giovanni and Tobias remained for the present on their own ship. Passing from one vessel to the other was not easy because of the rough seas about the reef; yet the men were evidently well-practised in such operations.

As the party reached the deck, some of the shipwrecked people began explaining volubly what had happened. When the disaster befell them, in the middle of the night, they lowered their boat and fought each other to get into it. Too many forced their way aboard, amid yells and fisticuffs, and all was turmoil down there among the foaming seas, so far as could be heard; almost nothing could be seen in that black night. Suddenly a gigantic wave rolled in, engulfing the overloaded craft and those aboard her as they shrieked and struggled for their lives. All perished in a moment, devoured by the sea and the darkness, the only survivors being those who had failed to find room in the boat—those who had lacked strength enough to force their way into it. Also the master, who refused to leave his ship. But the rest of the crew had abandoned her, and by their great bodily strength succeeded in making room for themselves, as did many others—all except those who now remained and who for the most part were peaceable merchants, unused to such ghastly adventures as this. They now thanked god that they had been left behind to perish and, on that very account, had not perished, but through the inscrutable grace of god had been rescued in their great distress.

The skipper listened to their account with a sullen air, betraying no particular interest in their circumstantial narration. When they had finished he told them curtly to hand over their money; he would accept it in return for rescuing them. No money, no rescue.

They looked at him blankly, and showed no sign of obeying his order.

"Didn't you hear me?" he demanded sharply. "You surely don't imagine I'm going to save you for nothing? Bring out all the money you have and all other valuables. And be quick about it!"

They stood thunderstruck, first from amazement, then from fright and the dread of losing their possessions. Some stammered that they had nothing, and at these the skipper smiled in derision, remarking that this was hardly likely since they were so well-dressed; nor had he ever heard of merchants lacking in worldly possessions. So far as he knew, such men were always well-furnished with money. But he was not going to wait here all day. Unless it was handed over at once, he and his men would take it for themselves.

"And anyhow," said he, turning to a man of a different aspect from the rest, "the ship's funds will be handed over to me. You, I fancy, are master of this vessel. Or rather *were*. She has become a wreck and I've taken lawful possession of her. Go below and bring up the strong-box, as I ordered you."

The man he addressed was elderly, grey-haired, rather fat but powerfully built, with a strong face and a resolute look in his honest seaman's eyes. Those eyes expressed no particular regard for the colleague who was now giving him orders. Nevertheless, without a word, he went below.

Meanwhile the merchants began to negotiate for acceptable terms. Of course they wished to recompense their rescuers for their trouble—for their almost inestimable services—but within reasonable limits. What sum did they suggest, they enquired, in the traditional trading manner.

The skipper replied that there was now no question of any bargain: their very lives were at stake. And when this was so a man paid not this sum or that, but all he had. *All. Now* did they understand?

The merchants were outraged. They seethed with indignation and clearly had no intention of submitting. Anything—yes, death itself—was preferable to the loss of all they possessed. If they must choose—if it really had come to that—their possessions were dearer to them than anything. They were men of peace, indeed, but not at any price, and some things were dearer to them than life. If these shameless extortioners insisted that there could be no question of bargaining, they would answer that their honour as traders was here involved and that they refused to stomach such an insult to their respectable profession; they would show that they were men of honour and courage who would yield to no one in defence of themselves and their property.

At this point the master reappeared at the hatchway, without the strong-box but armed with cutlass and knife and carrying other weapons. These he quickly distributed among his passengers, who snatched them without delay and began wielding them to the best of their ability against their so-called rescuers, whom they now perceived to be no better than brigands. In an instant all were engaged in a violent hand-to-hand struggle on the slanting deck; for those from the pirate ship at once responded by drawing the weapons they had held concealed in their clothes, and closing with the merchants. The skipper, their leader in the struggle, issued brief, decisive commands like the cracks of a whip, and exhorted the giant and Ferrante to attack now here, now there, now in one fashion, now in another, in the confused battle in which he himself, strangely enough, took scarcely any part. Yet with eyes that at other times were so indifferent he was quick to observe all that happened, supervising and following the progress of the contest calmly and with seeming unconcern, and directing his men with his thin but penetrating voice.

Ferrante indeed needed few orders; he was evidently experienced and skilled in such affairs as this, and his contemptuous smile showed that it gave him satisfaction and pleasure. Curiously enough he seemed more inclined to throttle his victims than to cut them down; he snatched at their throats with his long, hairy, clawlike, rapacious hands, and not until that failed did he resort to the knife. It was a long narrow knife with a point like a needle that the victim saw moving before his eyes before it stabbed. Ferrante executed his horrid handiwork alone and in his own peculiar manner.

The clumsy and perhaps rather simple-minded giant, on the other hand, needed all the leadership he could get. He was like a sluggish mass that required some impulse to set it moving, but once he started he was terrible indeed. The difficulty was to arouse his savagery and force him to overcome his natural good-humour. He tried to behave as if he were angry, but in fact he was not. At the beginning this was very evident; so it was the more remarkable that, by means of the whip, the skipper was able to work him up into true berserk fury. The results were appalling, because of his enormous strength. He felled his adversary instantly with his huge fists, and then hurled himself upon him with his knife, bending over the victim like a burly butcher. It was terrible to see: his eyes protruded, his great mouth with its fleshy lips gaped wide and panted with his strained breathing; his hairless scalp flushed red with excitement. But when he stood up, his victim dealt with, he smiled almost benevolently for a moment before hurling himself at the next.

During this wild mêlée little Giusto kept as far as possible in the background. He felt out of place and would have preferred to slink away and hide. He was like a little mouse that would rather scuttle off when the big rats are biting. His almost complete inactivity—despite the long knife that he carried, like the rest—did not escape the skipper's keen eye, and from time to time he cast an irate glance at him; yet this did not overcome Giusto's innate cowardice and fear. Giusto was more afraid of the captain than of anything; nevertheless in this he did not obey him.

Thus only two of the pirate's party were actually fighting, but being better skilled at the business and superior in physique, they held their own against all who opposed them and who, although spurred on by the courage of despair, were too little accustomed to violence to survive for long. At one moment the outcome seemed uncertain, and observing this the skipper called to Giovanni and Tobias to come up and help. It was not clear whether he meant both, or Giovanni alone. Giovanni took a few steps towards the ladder that still hung from the wreck, then halted, casting a shy, silent glance at Tobias, who had not stirred and who remained staring out to sea, his tense, hard face betraying no sign of the turmoil in his mind.

It was the master of the wrecked vessel who gave most trouble. For all his age he was incomparably the strongest of their adversaries, and well used to exerting his strength in all manner of ways when need arose. Indeed they did not gain the upper hand of him until all the rest lay either dead or severely wounded and bleeding on the deck, and he resisted violently until the very end. "You hyena!" he roared, foaming with rage at the skipper as he aimed a cut at him, which however wounded him only slightly, for Ferrante threw himself between them. At last they succeeded in binding him with a rope, and with that the fight was over.

The skipper ordered Ferrante and the giant below, to examine the cargo and note what items were most valuable and easiest to transfer to their own ship. Then he summoned little Giusto, who approached timidly, fearing the worst. Ferrante wanted to stay and finish off the master, but the skipper waved him and the giant away. "We'll see to this," he said.

Their victim lay bound and unable to stir. Nor did he say anything now, but merely glared contemptuously at his victorious foe. It was this contempt that so greatly infuriated the pirate skipper, and not without reason he suspected the other of regarding him as a commander of a lower order altogether. Hate gleamed in his reptilian eyes, and with it the desire to be revenged upon this worthy old man, who fancied himself superior because he commanded a so-called honourable vessel, laden with traders and with wares that were bought and sold in a so-called honourable manner; to be revenged upon all this honesty and upon this man with the grey hair and candid seaman's eyes, which at the moment were neither calm nor candid, but as wild as an animal's.

"Did you call me a hyena?" he asked, speaking very slowly. "Is that what you said?"

The master made no reply, having evidently resolved to engage in no conversation with his despised executioner.

"Then I'll show you how a hyena sets about his prey. He doesn't kill it himself, as you may know. He doesn't deign to, or perhaps it doesn't amuse him. He leaves that to someone else.

"Come here!" he said to Giusto. "Come closer! Are you scared, you poor wretch? Can't you see the man's tied up, fast and firm? You've got nothing at all to be afraid of.

"Here's this cowardly little fellow who will take care of you. He may not be very clever at it, but he'll pull it off in the end.

"Now then, Giusto—show yourself a man! Stop shivering, you little runt! Begin!"

Giusto's face was white. He was indeed trembling, and the long narrow knife that resembled Ferrante's looked far too big in his small hand. The point quivered incessantly.

"Now! Stab him! Stab him, I tell you!"

Giusto bent over the victim and aimed several blows, but they seemed barely to pierce his clothes.

"You miserable wretch, can't you do it? Go for his throat, then—his throat!"

Giusto obeyed; but when the blood spurted forth he turned green in the face and broke out into a cold sweat. He could not endure the sight of blood. And the skipper, who was well aware of this, took especial pleasure in compelling him. His voice rang out in cold command above the little fellow, who cowered over his victim and was by far the more terrified of the two. During all this time the old man uttered no sound, and this self-control seemed to exasperate his slayer still further.

"Cut his throat! Cut his throat!" he cried hoarsely, his own self-control completely gone.

Giusto dared not do as he was ordered but, half-closing his eyes, he struck blow after blow at the man's neck with his over-large knife until at last, despite his clumsiness, he had carried out his task and put the man to death. By then the victim was drenched in blood, and over him crouched Giusto, vomiting, his face deathly white and his forehead wet with sweat.

Satisfied at last, the skipper stood laughing at him and the dead man.

Thus did he torture at one and the same time the

poor old fellow with the honest face and the terrified little rat who slew him.

Now Ferrante and the giant came up through the hatch bearing two big bales; the giant's was huge, for he liked best to carry really heavy things. They did not know what the bales contained, and for this the skipper cursed them. Then he ordered Giusto to go below and see what there was of real value, and most suitable for them. In these matters he relied chiefly on the little man, whom in all else he deeply despised.

But first he wanted to go through the traders' pockets, to discover what they might be carrying, and Giusto—much relieved, very thankful and eager to engage in his regular occupation—immediately applied himself to this. Deftly and swiftly he searched both the quick and the dead, and collected a great quantity of cash, which the skipper at once impounded. Those who were yet alive moaned in lamentation when he touched them and stripped them of their earthly possessions, but they made no further resistance.

After that he followed Ferrante and the giant below, to continue the plundering of the wreck.

Transferring the cargo took some time, and the

giant and Ferrante made many trips between the wreck and their own vessel, although Giusto saw to it that only the best and least bulky objects were taken. He came upon a great deal that was worth stealing, and ran repeatedly up on deck, in delight, to report his finds to the skipper. He was always delighted by a good haul, although he was never allowed to keep any of it, nor given so much as a word of thanks. In a way he was a very unselfish person, and therefore happy. He was now especially happy because they had captured so rich a prize.

Was he not almost a good man? But such questions are always hard to answer.

Last of all the giant carried across some great wine-casks and barrels of various sorts, which the skipper—with some reluctance—allowed them to take.

Then they made ready to cast off.

Groans and cries of distress could still be heard from those merchants who were yet alive. Tobias went up to the skipper and exhorted him to take these men with him, but the skipper looked at him in derision without deigning to reply. He merely shrugged his shoulders and turned his back. Ferrante, who was standing near by, uttered a dry, scornful laugh, and shot a ferocious glance at Tobias.

Then they set sail.

It was sunset. The sea, which was almost calm, shimmered in many colours: hazy, fleeting colours of indescribable beauty, as if flowers of every kind had been scattered over its boundless surface, to rock upon it until they slowly faded, paling away in a death of ineffable bliss, melancholy and loveliness.

Tobias stood quite alone, watching.

They had reason to be pleased with themselves and their prize. Even the skipper seemed content. He could not deny that they well deserved a bumper, and allowed them to broach a cask and sit down on deck to eat and drink. They had earned and no doubt needed a good square meal; and food there was in plenty—far finer food than they were used to. Ferrante and the giant threw themselves upon it with a voracious appetite, the giant especially devouring huge quantities, shovelling loads into his great mouth and washing them down with floods of wine. He seemed somehow to eat and drink with his whole body; watching him, one understood whence he derived his enormous muscles and his strength, and how he had become what he was and how he would so remain. It was like watching, as it were, his coming into being and his continued existence. But it was probably not often that he had the opportunity to gorge himself in this fashion.

Ferrante ate more like an ordinary person, with a greed that was natural after so many varied labours. He ate with a sombre fury—angrily, as he did everything. Both drank great quantities of wine which soon took effect on Ferrante. But the giant was one who could never get intoxicated however much he drank. He did his best now, but failed, and he looked with envy at the others as they grew tipsier and tipsier. Already it was clear to him that as usual he, the only sober one, would be taking the helm that night.

Giusto ate very little and put only tiny morsels into his small, pale mouth, yet he seemed to delight all the more in what he did take. He beamed and revelled, wholeheartedly content with himself and all the world. He drank too, to be like the others and to persuade Ferrante, whom he greatly admired, that he was drinking as much as Ferrante himself. In fact, however, he had so weak a head that he was overcome almost at once, and in a ludicrous manner: his little ratface was ill-suited to such a fiery-red and fuddled aspect. He laughed continuously, with a half-witted, clucking laughter as if he were a hen, his Adam's apple running up and down his scrawny bird's throat; and his little eyes radiated a doltish bliss, although really he was the most astute of all those men.

The skipper too sat with them, but as if not of them. He took no part in their talk and uttered no word. He ate, however, and above all drank a great deal; in time he must have become blind drunk. Yet he betrayed nothing of this and underwent no apparent change. His chill, reptilian eyes seemed incapable of kindling and he observed the other men and their inebriated behaviour with his usual cold, contemptuous look. When they said anything more than usually foolish he laughed scornfully at what had tickled them. Thus he had little joy either of them or of his own potations. He soaked in solitude and without mirth, so that it might be wondered why he did it at all. But no less might one wonder why he did so much else just as gloomily; and why people in general do things in which they surely can take no pleasure. Yet perhaps they can?

Dusk was falling, and they had hung a lantern from a spar to see by and to continue feasting. It was a warm evening; the wind had dropped entirely and they stayed where they had first sat down. In time all except the giant had become so drunk that the mood of the company altered somewhat. As might be imagined, Ferrante was not cordial in his cups, and having glared first at one and then another he seemed set on girding at the skipper. He showered him with jibes and spiteful innuendoes, veiled hints and questions as to just how much he made out of the ship, how much he had pocketed this time in cash alone, and how much of it he was going to share with them.

A great deal was needed to embolden him to speak so, for even he was afraid of the skipper—the man who had so singular a power to inspire fear. At other times these two stood by each other more than the rest, if any aboard could be said to do so. They felt a kind of mutual respect, and Ferrante was the only one whom the skipper did not altogether despise. But this topic was a perilous one, and it was not the first time that Ferrante had broached it after drinking too much.

Giusto listened, very unhappy. He dared not raise

his eyes. Of course Ferrante was right; men such as he and the giant were worth any sum, and the skipper undoubtedly kept too much for himself. But it was a pity that they had begun to talk of it: what good would it do? For his own part he laid no claim to anything, nor did the others dream that he might; neither he nor they regarded Giusto as a true member of this crew. He desired nothing; he was satisfied with board and lodging, as it were, and with being to some extent one of the rest. Giovanni, too, cared little for pay or a share in the winnings so long as he had enough to make a beast of himself in port; and indeed he was of no use in a tight place, though good at the routine work on board, of course, being strong and able. And this new fellow—who was he? And by the way, where were the two of them now? They weren't drinking with the others. Or perhaps they were although he didn't see them; he wasn't taking in much at this stage, he knew, and not clearly, being so drunk.

Then he saw Ferrante rising to his full height, tall and sinewy, and swaying a little as if in the wind, and to his horror he beheld him shaking his fist at the skipper. What would come of this? He hardly dared watch.

The skipper also rose, to stand face to face with Ferrante, bending upon him a gaze of icy, sneering contempt for him and for all other men without exception. Ferrante broke off in the middle of a coarse jibe, cowed by this unnaturally cold look—as an exacerbated wild beast is cowed in the very act of roaring at his tamer—though he was much the stronger of the two, and his eyes were bloodshot with fury. The clenched fist dropped and the tall, gangling man stood open-mouthed, so that one could see the gap on the left side of his lower jaw, from which three teeth were missing. With a few flinging, aimless motions of his long body he squirmed away into the darkness.

Their banquet broke up. Giusto, too, took the opportunity of slinking off, thankful that there had been no fight and that he might sleep off his little carousal in peace and quiet. The giant followed him noisily below, since no one had given him any orders and the air was so still that it could make no difference whether anyone stood at the helm or not. At last the skipper, too, went below to sleep off his desolate bout.

The deck lay quiet, empty and deserted, or so it seemed.

Suddenly Giovanni, who was at the helm and had been there all the time, spied a lanky figure stealing forward amidships, on the port side, towards the place where Tobias was probably sleeping. He heard a half-stifled cry, left the tiller and hurried forward.

He arrived in time to see Ferrante's long, hairy hands grasping Tobias' throat like sharp talons; another moment and Giovanni would have been too late. Dashing up he dragged the madman backwards, caught him by the shoulders and flung him to the deck.

A long, slim knife glinted in the hand of the prostrate man; Giovanni stooped, wrenched it from him and tossed it into the sea.

What made him do that? Had he acted deliberately or on impulse?

The knife was bloodstained, but in the depths it would be cleansed. As everything must be at last.

Certainly it was there, into those depths, that Ferrante had meant to throw his victim after the murder, and so wipe out all trace. That is, if he could think so far in his present frenzy. After his humiliating defeat by the skipper his rage had sought another outlet and turned against this newcomer whom he already detested as he had detested Giovanni before him. Were they to have yet another good-for-nothing aboard who did nothing to earn his keep? Wasn't it enough to carry the one they said had been a shaveling? That fellow, too, he would like to leave his mark upon and show him he wasn't wanted here. It would have been just as easy.

But now he himself lay beaten, and that elderly man of god had proved the stronger of the two; he had conquered and disarmed him.

"Get up and be off!"

And Giovanni launched an ungentle kick.

"Off with you below!"

Ferrante rose and reeled away, down below deck to join the others.

Tobias and Giovanni stood side by side in the darkness, which was no true darkness, for the sky was full of stars.

They had avoided one another, and had had every occasion to do so; but now here they were together. And one had saved the other's life.

Much had happened since morning and that vital conversation—since Giovanni had talked so much about the sea. The holy sea—in which Ferrante's knife was now sinking and sinking, leaving its blood in that dark embrace and becoming cleansed.

54

To surrender to the sea—the great and endless sea which is indifferent to all things, which erases all things; which in its indifference forgives all things.

Primeval, irresponsible, inhuman. Freeing man through its inhumanity, making him irresponsible and free—if he will only choose the sea and surrender to it.

How long ago, how remote was this talk that they had had together! How long it seemed since Giovanni had uttered those strange words which came as a revelation and seemed to open up a whole new world! How long ago ...

Now, as the knife sank and sank, Tobias asked him how he could have chosen this life—how he could ever have chosen it. And how he could endure it.

Giovanni did not answer at once. Instead he walked slowly aft and lashed the tiller. The other man followed. There was really no need to lash it, for there was no wind and one could scarcely detect any forward movement of the ship. Yet he did what was customary.

And when he had done it he lay down on the deck with his big hands under his head and looked up at the night sky with all its burning stars. Was he preparing to sleep?

For a while Tobias stood beside him; then he too lay down. They remained there beside each other in the warm night.

It was a flat calm and the ship glided imperceptibly forward, or perhaps was not moving at all. No matter: she was bound for no goal. She merely reposed upon the sea, the infinite sea.

Then Giovanni began to tell of something that no one had ever heard him tell before.

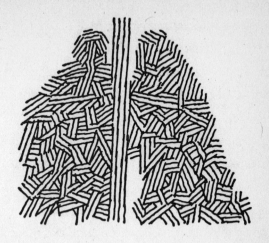

I GREW UP in a very pious home. My mother was a widow and I was her only child. My father died before I was born and I was brought up by this solitary woman who was no longer young and who perhaps after my father's death turned even more fully to god for consolation and support.

From the very beginning, when she gave birth to me in her loneliness, she determined that my life should be dedicated to god. To the church and to god. *She* decided this. I could hardly have been consulted at that time, nor was I ever asked later about a matter of such decisive importance to me. But she acted from a deep love for me and from concern for my soul's salvation and my eternal good, of which she was thinking even then.

I was her only possession and she gave me away— to god. She consigned me to the safest, surest embrace she knew: to her lord and saviour. And to draw his attention to me and bind me truly to him she gave me the name of Giovanni, after the disciple he loved most.

Often and often did she explain this to me, impressing upon me that I bore a holy name, and the reason for it.

I own that I saw nothing remarkable in this, and was quite of her opinion. It was to god and to no one else that I was to consecrate my life. I was filled with the same piety as herself—with the same love for him and for that son of his who suffered and who hung crucified in all the rooms of our house. During my childhood and youth my mind was altogether turned away from this world and bent upon holy things— upon that world where the divine lived its serene and tranquil life.

I must own, too, that it was a happy time for me— that my childhood and adolescence were really happy

—when I think now of my later life and of human existence in general. I was surrounded by a great peace, and within myself there was always peace. I had security and complete certainty about everything, and I was perfectly satisfied with my world, with the loving embrace in which my mother had placed me and with my repose in god.

Nor did I feel that world to be enclosed and narrow; had anyone suggested such a thing I would have been mystified. On the contrary, to me it seemed rich and vast—indeed infinite. Thoughts of the heavenly father and of his son born here on earth, of his bright realms, and of the body that bled on Golgotha, seemed to open a boundless universe before my enraptured gaze. Mine was a burning faith, and this faith enlarged my world far beyond its earthly frontiers.

Thus for me our stifling, narrow little home, where an ordinary youngster could not have breathed and where in every room an emaciated man hung dying for our sake, was full of meaning—part of the greatest possible whole—in which without any sense of restraint one might grow up and await one's vocation.

The city in which we lived was not large, yet it

was renowned far and wide for its many churches; the cathedral was especially famous for its beauty and its sacred relics. There were relics, too, in some of the other churches, and the place was a place of pilgrimage to which many people came to pray and to seek the consolations of religion.

There was also a seminary for priests, which in due course I entered, after instruction by the fathers in the convent school. I was entrusted to their care and received into the bosom of the church; and this was no more than a continuation of my home and of my earlier life. I was a most willing and interested pupil, eager to listen and to learn from them all that so fully occupied my young mind. I always pursued my studies to their entire satisfaction; my mother heard much in my praise and, during the latter part of my studies, their repeatedly expressed hopes of me and my future.

At last came the great day—surely the greatest of her life—when I was ordained priest.

For me, too, this was a great and notable day; I was profoundly moved to be standing before god's countenance as his servant, and filled with a burning desire to serve him in truth, from love of my calling.

Soon afterwards I was appointed chaplain at one

of the churches in the town—one of the lesser ones, certainly, but the very oldest and in fact the most beautiful of them all. With its ancient vaulting, only faintly seen by the light falling through the archaic stained-glass pictures of the lives of the saints, it was filled with the spirit of sanctity, with dimness and illumination, with the complexity of the divine and its enigmatic, mysterious power.

I remember it very well. But I remember also the incense there—that sweet, sickly fragrance that ever pervaded that most venerable temple.

At the time, of course, I never noticed that familiar smell. I loved the old church very much and felt happy that I had been called upon to work within its walls.

I must have served there for some months when the thing happened.

One day I was summoned to hear confession, and learned that the penitent was a woman. Actually another priest, some years older than myself, would have heard it, but since he had suddenly fallen ill he asked me to deputise for him.

It was evening, and because I had been summoned

late I arrived a little after the appointed time. It was then almost dark inside the church; only at one of the altars were candles burning before the statue of the madonna. No one was there but the woman, whom I at once perceived near the confessional. I greeted her perfunctorily without getting much of an impression of her, other than noticing that she was veiled. There was nothing strange or particularly unusual about that. Then we immediately went into confession.

I had never confessed anyone before, and so I wondered rather how it would be—how I should behave and what I should say to the person who sought guidance and penance of me, who was so young. I myself of course had made my confession regularly and often to our family confessor, so that in that respect I was on familiar ground. Still, I must own that I had had woefully little experience, never having had anything of moment to confess. My sins, and my efforts to find something important to say, had often brought a smile to my confessor's lips.

I bent towards the grille to listen.

She had a low, warm voice, and she spoke with intense emotion from the beginning. It was some time before I really grasped what she was saying. Moreover, it seemed to me that she expressed herself confusedly; perhaps because at first she was reluctant to speak plainly of what burdened her heart.

After a while I gathered that she was speaking of one she loved but ought not to love. For what reason she ought not I failed to understand; and the very reason for her confession confounded me because of my utter inexperience. Nor, as I said, did she express herself clearly or frankly. Yet over and over again she declared that her love was sinful—a great transgression which she must acknowledge to someone because she could no longer bear the burden of her wicked secret.

When I asked her outright why her love was sinful she owned that, as I had suspected, she was married; for some years she had been joined in matrimony to another man, so that her love was an offence against god and his holy sacrament, her sin a mortal sin.

It was a terrible thing for her to know this and at the same time to be incapable of putting a curb upon her feelings. It rent her asunder—she was torn by conflict and self-reproach. She was a deeply religious woman who desired to be pure and worthy of honour; the sharper therefore were the pangs of conscience inflicted by this wild obsession. All her thoughts were of her beloved; all day they centred upon him alone and at night he never left her, though he was never with her, and he continually engrossed her fevered imagination. She was possessed by blind passion, and yet aware that unless she could conquer it, it would prove her downfall and deprive her soul of salvation.

Was she to sacrifice bliss and eternal life for a passion—an emotion—here on earth, during her brief and negligible mortal span?

She herself knew the answer—she knew what alone was of true worth. Her soul, fighting for salvation, knew the answer. But within her some other force struggled and protested, refusing to sacrifice itself or submit; refusing to be stifled by her longing for eternal bliss. It craved its bliss now, at this moment, if only for an instant in this fleeting earthly life, and would then willingly burn to all eternity in the fires of hell. It sought to hurl her to perdition, caring nothing for her or for her fate in another world.

Thus was she torn by conflicting emotions, and knew not what to do in her distress. Even then at that very moment, as she tried to explain her misery and sought comfort in the sacred act of confession, the battle raged on within her. She could not crush it, could not stifle the fire—hell-fire—not even now during this utterly sincere acknowledgment of her sin before god. The words on her lips declared and condemned her transgression; the lips themselves yearned for it.

Such was her confession: the first I had ever heard. I listened. She alone spoke.

Her low, fluttering voice sounded very clear in the utter silence that surrounded us, and I had no further difficulty in catching what she said: not a word escaped me. Also she spoke frankly now, very much more frankly than at first. Sometimes her voice sank almost to a whisper because of her reluctance to give herself away, yet I heard it without effort—that warm, agitated voice of hers that pleaded for help and succour; every word, every gasp reached me; and all the time, through the grille, I felt her hot breath.

I sat there in the darkness of the cramped confessional and listened, bending forward with clasped hands as no doubt she was doing beyond those bars, while she testified to her sin.

When she ended there was silence. Now it was for me to speak, but I knew not how to answer. My inexperience left me at a loss. At last I stammered that I well understood her great distress, her torment and dread—and added such other phrases as occurred to me: empty words that could be of little help to her. I exhorted her to pray; I spoke of the power of prayer to withdraw one's thoughts from sin; I urged her to turn her whole mind to god, and he would surely receive a soul so eager for salvation. With god our thoughts found peace, for he was their true home.

She replied that she had tried by every means to do so, but that god was as if absent; love and the beloved alone existed.

After these words silence fell once more.

Then I told her that I would pray for her, pray that god might allow her supplication to reach him. And it was agreed that we would unite in prayers for her soul.

With that this strange confession was at an end and we stepped out from the confessional.

For a moment I saw her figure as she walked away through the dimness of the church, to the holy-water stoup by the door, and then out. There the veiled head was silhouetted more plainly because it was lighter outside than where I was standing.

On my way home I felt most displeased with myself. It seemed to me, and rightly, that I had been a very bad confessor and of no use whatever. How was she helped, in her agony and need, by my well-meaning counsels which, sound though they might be, could not touch her troubled life—her turbulence—or alter anything at all? She was abandoned to her fate, to her blind and, to me, incomprehensible passion, as completely when she left me as when she came. I had had no power to release and help her; I had merely repeated familiar, hackneyed phrases without fire, without living content. There was nothing strange in that, for they had held no living content even for me; there was no fire in myself, such as there should be in a true spiritual guide. Such a one I had never been and perhaps never would be.

Only in her had there been fire; not in the man who should save her, rescue her from perdition—from sin. No, I was far from satisfied with myself.

I suspect it was all because I was so young.

I went home through the dark streets greatly cast

down and full of an inner perturbation such as I had never known.

After I was in bed I remembered my promise to pray for her; to pray that god might deliver her from the sinful love that possessed her. I tried to inject as much ardour into my prayer as I could and make it as glowing and passionate as a prayer ought to be—and as hers surely was: the one that was not accepted by god . . .

Strange that it should not be accepted, whereas mine . . . Yet it was she and not I who was in need.

For her, god did not exist, while I spoke familiarly with him every day.

But this terrible thing had a particular cause— the fact that for her, only her beloved existed. Only love existed.

I prayed as ardently as I had ever prayed, yet I could not feel that my prayer was heard, as I usually did. Or did I? I'd never given it much thought, perhaps, and took it for granted that god heard me.

What did I really know about my prayers? How could I tell that they were accepted? How could I be so sure?

I lay for a long time pondering and questioning

myself, and ideas that had never before entered my head now troubled me.

For the first time I was questioning myself rather than god.

A week had barely passed when I had word that the same woman wanted to come to confession again. This time, too, she had asked for the older priest, but he still lay sick and asked me to take his place.

I was curiously agitated by this message, although in itself it was unremarkable.

Why was this? I could make nothing of it.

Throughout that day—throughout the time of waiting until the hour of confession—I remained in the same strange state of excitement.

Again she did not come until the evening, evidently to avoid observation; and again she was veiled. No doubt she was known to many in the town, though not to me; owing to my isolated life I knew very few there. She may have belonged to some respected family. At least she was not a woman of the people: that could be seen from her dress, which was of a distinguished simplicity only found among the higher classes of society, and not often there.

She was certainly very anxious not to be recognised, and no doubt it was for this reason that she had chosen this little church, which few attended, and which may also have appealed to her because of its age, beauty and atmosphere and because it seemed a suitable place for a woman of her temperament to make confession.

Once more, in the dusk, we entered the confessional.

She began by thanking me for being allowed to return. Her confession had helped her; she had found relief in unburdening herself and in no longer bearing her trouble alone. She also felt that in spite of everything she was not quite cut off from the consolations of religion.

I held my breath as I listened, fearing to lose a single word. As before, she spoke very softly, and I had to lean close to the grille to hear her soft, warm voice expressing humble gratitude which I in no way deserved. If she had felt some relief, some comfort, it was god who had permitted it, who had bestowed it, not his worthless servant—the most worthless and unsuitable confessor she could have found. If he had heard anyone's prayer it was hers—that sincere prayer from an agonised heart—not my lukewarm petition, without passion or ardour, and altogether lacking in the power of a true and experienced shepherd of souls to guide and give support along the path to god.

But these thoughts I kept to myself, of course. I remained silent, waiting for her to say more.

She went on to declare that she had nevertheless undergone no change, none whatever; she was still filled with this love that was forbidden and hopeless and yet ruled her and held her fate in its hand. The solace she had felt had no effect upon this and never could. For in truth she did not want to be delivered from these wicked feelings, rescued from the consuming, hopeless passion that possessed her and by which she desired to be possessed. So it was. That was the truth and she must frankly own to it. She did not *want* to be free! And how is one to save someone who does not want to be saved?

Nevertheless it had relieved her to speak out, to open her overburdened and tormented breast and candidly acknowledge her distress.

I noted that more than once she described her love as hopeless; she repeated this at least twice.

Why, I wondered, was it hopeless? Could it be that it was not returned? Did the object of it not share her feelings? Was it perhaps therefore unfulfilled, and not . . . I had difficulty in thinking of the purely physical aspect, and would have preferred not to do so; yet at the same time I found to my alarm that it lingered in my mind and greatly interested me and that I wanted to hear about it.

Warily and shyly I ventured upon this delicate subject, to gain clearer understanding. I did not know how to express myself, and was above all afraid of expressing myself too plainly.

She answered vaguely and evasively and seemed reluctant to speak of it. She slid away from the theme to some other one, and made no direct or definite reply.

We were both equally indeterminate in what we said—in our manner of avoiding decisive words—and I arrived at no clear understanding or certainty.

All the same I gained the impression that her passion was unrequited and was perhaps the more ardent on that account; that her love, which she called unlawful and a mortal sin, was an unhappy love—a love that found no response, even as her burning prayers to god found no response.

I was deeply moved by this and filled with compassion—and at the same time with a heat that took me by surprise and made me ashamed. So complicated were my feelings that I quickly dropped this subject which seemed as disturbing to me as to her. I stammered a few words that had no bearing on what I had been saying, to help me to drop the matter that must be painful to her and that I regretted having touched upon. Then I was silent.

It was strange to see how she herself behaved during the embarrassing silence after our talk about her hopeless and unfulfilled love, about the fact that she was alone with her passion, and with her thoughts that had been so painfully exposed.

She broke the silence with touching eagerness, in a way that eased us both. Lightly and airily as a bird, she fled from the tormenting thoughts that had been forced upon her against her will—fled to her beloved, to talk of him and describe him: those young, pure features that were ever before her, and the youthful purity of his soul that was so different from others! She spoke of her constant awareness of his presence although they could seldom meet; of how alive he was to her—too much alive, too insistent—of how his embrace made her heart bleed and of how much pain he caused her, though she endured it gladly for the sake of her love—their love. And she told how she always carried his portrait in a locket at her breast, close to her troubled heart, so as to have him always near her; how she kissed it whenever she was alone and in the solitude of night, in the darkness. The darkness did not matter, for she knew the portrait so well that she did not need to look at it. Often, indeed usually, she did not open the locket, but kissed that instead of the picture, with closed eyes and her lips to his. Just as two lovers kiss with eyes closed because they have no need to see each other and because nothing must disturb their experience of love—of oneness. Was it not so?

"Yes, yes," I whispered. "So it is."

Through the grille I could feel her breath . . . mine too was hot, and I was panting. Our breaths met through the grille . . . and I seemed to catch the scent of her mouth, the mouth I had never seen and never would see—I seemed to be seeing it because of that fragrance . . .

Suddenly she broke off and burst into tears.

Her sobbing cut me to the heart, and I was on

the point of doing everything, anything I could to comfort her, when I heard her hurriedly leaving the confessional and speeding away over the old tombstones in the floor of the church, out into the dusk of evening. I watched her disappear, and remained standing, alone.

I knew now what had happened to me: I had been seized by the passion of which she had talked so much. All my thoughts circled about her—her alone; for days she obsessed me, whether during my duties or when reading the daily office—whatever I might be doing. At night she bereft me of sleep, for she never left me but lived continually in my inflamed imagination. I was as if possessed by her, helplessly delivered into her power: a woman I'd never seen, of whom I knew almost nothing and of whose identity I had no idea. All I knew was that she loved another man and that her burning love for him was unrequited; and that I, in my obsession with her sorrow, was filled with a kind of joy.

With astonishment—almost alarm—I perceived how my passion was changing me. Nothing mattered to me any longer, nothing that until then had made up my life. Only she and love existed. My former self, that pale, worn youth in my mother's house—in the rooms where hung the image of the crucified—was a stranger to me. The home in which I had been brought up and where my soul had been dedicated to god became a prison in which, since my mouth had whispered those great words of love—"Yes, yes; so it is"—I could scarcely breathe. After those words, how could I endure the house of the crucified?

I could no longer pray. And what good would it have done? My prayers would never have carried so far, never have been accepted. I had so offended against god that he would not have listened to me or have had anything more to do with me. My passion was truly criminal, for I had allowed myself to be overpowered by it during confession, holy confession, and with a penitent who had turned to me in trust, seeking through me god's guidance and support, and release from her sin. Yes, my offence against god was such that he must reject me.

Sometimes at night, when I could not sleep for my heated thoughts, I tried to pray; I tried to turn my mind to god and beg him to have mercy on me, to give me back my peace of mind and let me rest in him, in his arms, as before

Yet I knew that in my heart I did not want that peace of mind—I did not want what I was praying for. How then should he heed my prayer?

I did not yearn to rest again in the safety of god's embrace, in his light and peace. I wanted to burn in the fire of love.

Thus it was; this is what had happened to me. I had altogether changed into someone else because love had won mastery over me.

I had believed I loved my mother; I had taken it for granted, though in fact I had never given the matter a thought. I had believed—and with even more conviction—that I loved god, though I had not reflected upon that either.

Now I saw that I had never loved before.

But would I ever meet her again, or hear her voice? Would she ever come back? Why should she? There was no object in her visits and her confession: I had been unable to help her at all; and indeed last time she had even wept. When I thought of that I became so greatly troubled that the tears sprang to my own eyes.

The idea that I should probably never meet her again distracted me. How would I survive?

And unless she did return I could not meet her, for since I had no notion who she was I could not look for her, and were I to pass her in the street I would never even guess that it was she.

She ruled my destiny and was completely unaware of it.

I realised that if she did come back it would be to speak of her beloved, and so relieve her heart—her burdened, tortured heart. In this I placed my hope: that her heart would be oppressed, full of pain and grief.

I cared nothing for the reason of her coming: only that I might meet her and hear her voice again.

She had believed throughout, it seemed, that it was to the older priest she had been making her confession. For when at last she made a third request it was again he who received the message. He had by now recovered from his illness, but since I had twice taken his place he thought it best that I should continue to do so.

My breast felt as it would burst when very calmly
—with a quite unnatural calm—he told me this.

I arrived in good time. The church was not yet
entirely dark; a half-light prevailed, almost like that
of day. But gradually the darkness gathered beneath
the massive vaulting, and soon only the faintest of
evening light penetrated the dim windows with
their scenes from the lives of the saints. The pious
faces and deeply glowing garments faded, passed
into the night and were seen no more.

She did not come.

I was quite alone. No one else was there. Before
the image of the madonna six little candles were
burning, flickering in an imperceptible draught.
This may have come from the door, which as usual
stood ajar.

She did not come.

Restlessly I paced to and fro over the worn tombstones and their coats of arms and names of those
long since deceased, whose most fervent wish had
been to rest here. I walked and walked without
pause.

She did not come.

I grew ever more agitated.

At last I heard light, almost inaudible footsteps in the darkness by the door. Because of the darkness I could not see her at all.

But she had come.

I heard nothing and grasped nothing, nothing at all of what she said; I heard only her voice—her low, rather breathless voice—and felt her breath and the fragrance of her mouth—a woman's mouth . . . I seemed to see it before me in the darkness, soft and warm . . . the movement of her lips, how they parted, so that their fragrance reached me . . . a woman's fragrance. I experienced her as fragrance, as a message from a woman, a being altogether different from myself; an alien being for which I longed because it was alien, and because it was she . . . I longed for her alien lips, for the source of this fragrance that numbed me, deprived me of my senses— but with happiness, the happiness of being in her presence and of hearing once again her voice . . .

She fell silent.

I did not know what she had said, nor what I had answered—if I had answered at all. I did not think I had; I could only have listened, with quick-coming breath, through the grille. Our breath had met through the screen ... without words, without meaning to the words ... only lips moved, whispering to one another in their own language—their secret language—confiding in each other, as lips ...

And now she was gone—vanished in the darkness, out into the darkness again like a bird fleeing from its cage, silent and secret, unseen.

I hastened out into the night, out into the little square in front of the church. I heard footsteps ... steps that died away into a narrow street. I sped after them.

Some way along that street I caught up with her.

It was quite dark. I was guided by the footsteps alone; I recognised her by them, as I had heard them inside the church over the tombstones: her bird-light steps.

I too walked as lightly and silently as I could so as

not to attract her attention, or frighten her perhaps and make her think that she was being pursued.

But when I came up beside her she could not but notice that someone was walking there, whispering burning words of love in her ear: a voice in the darkness that could barely control itself for passion, choosing words that only one possessed by love could choose—softly-spoken words that hid their heat in the darkness, as embers try to hide themselves beneath the ashes so as not to frighten with their fire —their hidden fire. It seemed, too, as if she were not alarmed, not troubled by being accompanied along that narrow, deserted street in the night by someone she could neither see nor identify. She did not hasten her steps; on the contrary she walked rather more slowly than before . . . with bated breath . . . as if afraid that something in the situation might change.

"I knew you would come," she whispered, so low as barely to drown the beat of her heart. "How long you have been! But I knew you'd come at last. Beloved . . ."

She did not stop, yet she walked very slowly—even more slowly than before. We walked together gently, side by side.

"How did you know that I'd go home by this

street? I don't as a rule. But I didn't want to be seen. I've been to confession and confessed my secret love for you. How did you know? How could you guess? It's very strange. Surely love guided you, and guided you aright. Do you not think so?"

"Yes, yes," I whispered.

"Were you waiting for me outside the church? Did you think I'd be coming?"

"Yes . . ."

"I can understand. I realised you knew that I went there to confession—that it was there I confessed my love for you, and spoke openly of it to god. I have confessed everything. I told him, too, that I shall never be false to you, judge me as he may. He knows everything.

"Last time I thought I saw you in the darkness outside the church when I left it; you seemed to be standing a little way off. But you never came, you never followed me, and I knew then that it couldn't have been you.

"But now you *have* come; you've come at last . . . Beloved."

She tripped over the uneven paving; I held her gently under the arm and she leaned against me lightly.

"You may be wondering why I go to confession in that little church and not in the cathedral, where we belong," she continued. "But you see, I could never have spoken out frankly about this to Father Benedict, who's my regular confessor and who knows everything about our family—too much, indeed. But to this confessor at St. Thomas's, whom I don't know and who knows nothing about me— knew nothing about me—I could talk freely. To him I could lay bare my heart and give it into god's hand, just as it is. He has been of great help to me and I am grateful to him for his patience. But he is far too lenient: he has never yet uttered a harsh or condemning word, or laid any penance upon me. Indeed he has simply listened, and allowed me to speak from my overflowing heart. And allowed me to speak of you . . . And because I don't know him at all and have never even seen him—or he me— I've been able to do this; although as you know I'm reserved by nature and loth to confide in anyone.

"It was a help, too, that I was able to go there so late in the evening that no one saw me; I could speak more freely then and whisper words that I never dreamed could pass my lips. I have left my words there in the darkness, in the dusk within, as if entrusting them to that obscurity. The dimness under those old arches seems to suit our secret love so well, too; don't you think so?"

"Yes, I do."

Lightly she pressed my arm: I felt her slender hand upon it.

"And of course you'll have understood that I have another reason for choosing that particular old church for the confession of my love. So many of our ancestors, yours and mine, sleep there side by side, as you and I have longed to do. They sleep the last sleep, awaiting resurrection and the Judgment, as we too shall one day await it . . .

"I fear it. Yet at the same time—isn't it strange?— at the same time I long for the hour when I shall stand up and testify to my love—testify to you:

"'He is my beloved and without guilt,' I shall say. 'Look, Lord, upon the purity of his brow: he is not as the rest of us. I am the guilty one. And because of the miracle that I have been permitted to experience on earth I go willingly to the eternal punishment that I know must follow.'"

The street wound onward, narrow and dark, and now it began to climb; gently at first, then more sharply, becoming ever narrower and steeper until it was no more than an alley. We walked close-pressed to one another and her hand rested softly in mine. She had laid it there.

Neither of us said any more; not even she, who had said so much to fill my head with strange thoughts as I walked beside her in the night.

Up here stood the houses of the most eminent families, within whose palatial walls I had of course never been. But our narrow little alley was unlikely to lead to any of them.

All at once she stopped. I saw nothing, but with a hand that cannot have been so very strong she pushed open a low but massive door into a house, for I heard the creak of hinges and found that we were now in a narrow passage that smelt of mortar and damp. I felt her hand in mine; I felt her leading me along the pitch-dark passage and up an equally dark and narrow stair. At the top of this she must have opened another, quite silent, door, for now the smell of mortar and damp was gone and we were walking on a soft carpet that muffled our steps entirely. We were evidently in a room, a woman's room, for there was a faint fragrance which I imagined belonged to rooms inhabited by such beings. In a way it reminded me of the smell of incense in St. Thomas's, sweet and a little sickly, although at the same time it was very different.

I expected her to light a candle, but she did not, perhaps to avoid attracting attention in a house where there must certainly have been others besides ourselves—possibly many others; for although we had entered it by an inconspicuous little door in the alley, it might well be a large house: one of the old palaces in this upper part of the city.

Instead she softly put her arms about me and I felt her lips drawing near to mine, waiting for them, so close that I felt their warmth against my mouth as she caressed it lightly with her breath . . . Next moment we lost ourselves and became a single being, entwined into a single loving being that sank deeper and deeper into the bottomless well of love.

In my memory, that night is swathed in a warm dimness; I remember nothing else in quite the same way. I recall it not clearly but as something almost unreal—I recall it as a whole, as something deep down, as night. Although it's so long ago, it is still as much alive in me and I feel as if I had never experienced anything else. Through the warm darkness I hear her whisper in that well-remembered low, soft and rather trembling voice:

"Never leave my lips—never alone again—never again . . ."

We were both so famished that we seemed insatiable. Almost the whole night was spent in our assuagement, as again and again we made ourselves one.

Exhausted at last we fell asleep in close embrace, I think at the same time.

We did not wake at the same time, however.

Our awakening was in many ways so curious that I must describe it in some detail and perhaps at length, if it won't weary you too much.

I woke first, overflowing with a sense of happiness which at first I could not account for. Then I remembered, and in the somewhat harsh morning light that came in through the tall windows I saw her lying beside me naked, with her face upturned and her mouth half-open; her breathing was strained and laboured, with now and then a faint snoring. I was seeing her for the first time.

Perhaps she was not quite as I had imagined her:

not so very young and not altogether so beautiful. At the same time I realised that I had not formed any distinct image of her, however much my fancy may have played around her—or perhaps for that very reason. But I had not imagined her quite like that. She was very dark, with black hair curling down about her thin neck. Her mouth was narrow and pale, with the faintest suspicion of down on her upper lip, and there were shadows under her closed eyes—the result, it may be, of the night's exertions. No, she was not precisely beautiful, but there was a certain distinction in her somewhat over-long, over-lean face—a certain breeding. Her body was wonderful and not as thin as her face might have led one to expect: it was soft, almost plump, though slight, with small, fine-skinned, if not altogether youthful, breasts. I had nothing to compare it with, never having seen a woman's body before, but I was sure that it was marvellous. All women's bodies must be marvellous, I told myself.

I was not beautiful either, for that matter. As I lay looking own at my angular body I could find nothing attractive about it. I had never seen it before—not properly—not as I was seeing it now, when it had been put to its intended use, and so for the first time really existed.

My face could not have been called handsome either, emaciated and haggard as it was, with an unhealthy, somewhat pimply complexion from sitting so much indoors and poring over unworldly books. It's difficult to remember oneself as one was long ago, but that is how I see my face; and in it a pair of large eyes, hot with the fires that burned within my pallid, lanky young body.

Yet for all my lankiness I was powerfully built, and later developed into the big burly fellow you see now.

The bed on which we lay was covered with the finest linen, thinner and softer than any I had seen before, and the coverlet that we had tossed off in our passion was of costly material too, probably thick silk. The whole room, which was not large, was luxuriously appointed, and quite unlike anything I had ever seen.

But I did not care to examine it closely, nor did I have time, for now the woman beside me awoke— perhaps because in my gratitude to her luscious, sleeping body I had lightly and lovingly caressed it.

She stared at me with a look I have never forgotten. It was startled, amazed and horrified, all at the same time. And now I saw her eyes. They were large and very dark, timid and moist and slightly veiled like the eyes of a roe deer.

The horror in them no doubt arose from her discovery in the sober light of morning that it was not with her beloved that she had experienced the miracle of love, but with a stranger. Beside her lay a man whom she had never seen before, and it was with him that she had known that great miracle for which she had yearned so intensely. For she had surely known it; and perhaps awareness of this horrified her more than ever. I don't know. I only guess at what may have been going on in her mind as her eyes met mine—which were large too, like hers. And that, perhaps, was all we had in common. Who can say?

Her slender and most shapely hand, which during sleep had rested gracefully and as if protectively over her private parts, now moved slowly up to the locket that lay between her small, fine-skinned, if no longer youthful, breasts with the nipples that were too brown, and closed upon it as she continued to gaze at me with those big, scared roe deer eyes.

It was easy to divine what lay behind this gesture;

I understood only too well, and I was feverishly troubled by it—so greatly troubled as almost to surprise myself. Impulsively I put out my hand to snatch the locket with its portrait of the beloved whom she had so often talked of, so as to see what he looked like and who he really was. But beside herself with fright she stopped me and clenched her hand about it. The strength of that little hand in defence of her secret was extraordinary; I felt I could not have forced it open even if I had seriously tried —but in touching her and tussling against her warm little breasts my lust was again aroused, and was inflamed still more when she violently resisted me and tried with all her might to hold me off, so that I was more intent on that than on getting hold of the locket. She defended herself vigorously, but in the struggle her desire too awoke; suddenly she yielded and let me come to her; she drew me close to her, although I was not the right man—not the beloved, but a stranger—and we were fused in a wild ecstasy —wilder and fiercer just because of that—an ecstasy that brought even greater fulfilment than any during the night, and in a different way. Between her breasts against my own hairy breast I felt the locket with its portrait of her true love, the right one, he who was not like the rest of us, he with the pure brow, he of whom she would bear witness before god.

Afterwards she burst out weeping—a convulsive weeping—shaking all over, with her face buried in the pillow.

So our love began. Now for what came of it.

I visited her time and time again, stealing to her always by way of the narrow passage and up the equally narrow and obscure stairway. So far as I could tell, the little door from the alley was used by no one—no one but myself. The front of the palace —for it was indeed an old palace—was on the opposite side, overlooking a square, and in it was the main entrance, which I was careful to avoid. Mine was the stealthy way, unknown and unguessed-at by any: the murky passage smelling of mortar and damp, and so slippery that a man might slide on the greasy surface of the flagstones if he were not careful. One had to grope one's way forward, feeling with one's hand along the dripping wall. If this were not indeed a secret passage it became so, through me. It was only in the dark that I used it: in the evenings and later when I went home—when through the winding alley I had to walk warily lest anyone should spy me in my priestly garb at such an hour. If anyone did I hoped it would be thought that I was returning from a death-bed at which I had heard some poor soul's last agonised confession.

That such should be the path to our love was not surprising, for such was our love itself. Devious, shunning the light, kept secret at all costs from others: a stealthy love that must hide in its rat-hole —a rat-hole which was a luxuriantly-appointed room in a palace, yet nevertheless . . . I never beheld that room again, or never clearly, for we dared not kindle any but the faintest light lest we should be observed by the servants, who were to suppose that their mistress lay soundly asleep. And to stay until morning as on that first night when, exhausted by delight, we fell asleep in one another's arms, was something I dared not do again.

The dizzying peak of love was past, to be followed by the every-day of passion: passion self-nourished, fed by no new fuel. We were drawn, forced together by our desire, by our bodies' need for each

94

other. She had hungered so long in her marriage to the old man to whom she had been given in her tenderest youth—and with her locket between her ever more sagging little breasts. No wonder, then, that she yearned to be satisfied at last, even if not with the right man, the true beloved. Before it was too late. And I who had never before embraced a woman—never touched her warm skin or known the fragrance of her moist hairiness—had at last caught the scent of a female creature and was maddened by it and by the desire to smell it over and over again. Neither of us could break free from the other, questionable though everything was between us, and well though we understood the unlawfulness of our relationship. Now indeed we were committing a mortal sin: adultery not only in our hearts but fully consummated in the most shameful manner, in the very house of the deceived husband, between a confessor and his penitent—a sin to fill both god and man with abhorrence and condemn us both to hellfire. But to my astonishment I found that this only seemed to inflame my desire and pleasure, and render me yet more violent and insatiable.

What her feelings were I could not tell for certain,

though it was clear that she experienced something of the same kind. But she suffered too, in a way that I did not, and often as I rested in the peace of satisfied desire I heard her weeping softly beside me in the darkness. Sometimes she spoke of her beloved: of what he was like and of how terrible it would be if ever he came to know about this—about us. But that he, like her husband, did not care about her or want her was something she did not say. It was I who reminded her of that.

She went on insisting that I was quite strange to her—a complete stranger. She kept harping upon this. Yet she was no less a stranger to me. When first my passion was kindled I had never even seen her. And afterwards she was not as I had expected, not the one I had imagined and about whom I had woven my fancies. She of whom I had dreamt was different from the one who now lay beside me in bed, just as her true beloved in that locket between her breasts was someone different from me.

So we reproached and wounded one another and spoke harsh and cruel words. And when we parted it was not as two tender lovers usually do—or perhaps as lovers, but without tenderness.

This did not prevent us from meeting again. We both knew that we had to meet.

From the outset our love-relationship was based upon error, deception and conscious or unconscious falsehood, to an even greater extent than love in general. Everyday passion is more honest and candid, in that each tells the other the truth and helps him to tear down his illusions, even though it be often in a cruel and ruthless manner. The relationship between two people becomes more genuine and more sincere when there is less of love in it. This is bitter but, alas, true.

With us, however, our outward fraud increased; we were forced into more and more deception to keep our liaison a secret. It is strange how much one must lie once one has begun; how one must go on and on, whether one wants to or not, until one is enveloped in a tangled net of lies and half-truths which one can't even sort out oneself. One must lie over trifles, and things that have nothing to do with the real big lie. The original great falsehood may be fateful and fundamental, but the lies it entails can be absurdly trivial.

I had to lie and she had to lie, each in our own sphere. I to my old confessor and my brothers in office, who could not but observe the change in me and my growing indifference to my vocation and my duties as priest. Above all, of course, I had to lie to my mother. The woman had to lie to those who were about her daily: her husband and his family, her own family and their friends. Also to Father Benedict, her confessor. Her husband was the easiest to deceive, for after a long life of self-indulgence he now existed in a state of physical and mental decline in part of the old palace—which was similarly aged and decayed. Through other people, however, he might have found out what was going on—as in the end he did.

For me the most difficult thing was to conceal the matter from my mother. She must not discover my nocturnal absences: I had to wait until she slept and then steal out as silently as I could. But she became aware that something suspicious was afoot, and stayed awake—though feigning sleep—to spy upon me and my doings. On my return towards morning, too, she was often awake, I realised; she must have had little sleep. She pried into my affairs in her efforts to get on the scent, and her maternal instinct

—or whatever one may call it—soon led her to an awareness of what had befallen me and of the nature of my nightly ramblings. She began to interrogate me; she asked me sly, deceptive questions to which it was not easy to return convincing answers. I did my best but she would not be put off, and at last she worked out exactly what had happened.

Next she applied herself to discovering what woman it was who had ensnared her precious son in such diabolical toils. I don't know how she managed this, but she did. She betrayed herself by her inability to conceal her amazement that the despicable creature should come of so distinguished a family. This in no way modified her hatred or the evil expression it brought to her old face, which I noted with such astonishment. It was as if I had never really seen that familiar face before. Indeed I became aware of traits in my mother which I'd never before recognised, or to which I'd never paid enough attention. They must always have been there, of course, although their horrible manifestation had never until then been aimed at me, so that I had not been hurt by it; and in such cases we hardly notice the malice of those nearest to us.

Her wrath was now directed mainly against me. She showered me with jibes and vicious reproaches that most nearly resembled execration. Strangely enough she did not try to convert me, to persuade me to abstain from my hideous sin and find my way back to god. This may have been her intention, but she never said so. It was not her way, I think, to beg and plead. Instead she raged—threatened and raged —and invoked god's curse upon me, as if I had treacherously deprived her, or rather her god, of something that belonged to him—which indeed I had. Had she not handed me, her child, to god— into his loving embrace—instead of keeping me for herself? And now I had deprived god of that precious gift, so that his wrath must fall upon both me and her. She depicted for me all the agonies of hell—all that a priest, a man dedicated to god, might expect when he broke his holy vow of chastity and became a fornicator and adulterer: the worst thing imaginable, for which the devil was permitted to torture him to the utmost. She revelled in the thought of that torture. She presented me to the devil with the same ardent zeal as that with which she had once presented me to god: to his embrace as once to god's. To her own embrace she never invited me. She was as inhuman now as then, and I was struck by a thought that strangely enough had never crossed my mind before: when I was small she never treated me as a child—as her own quite ordinary little boy. I could not recall that she had fondled me, stroked my head or joked with me or pulled my ear or chucked me under the chin, or anything of that kind. I was always something special, always the chosen one—the chosen one of her and of god; the one to be presented, given away —to someone else. To Almighty God, for his use. To Him she had renounced her only child.

Now she gave me away to the devil.

Perhaps I never fondled her? I don't remember, and indeed I have never thought about it until this moment. So it may all be more complicated than I imagined.

She never encouraged it, though, and I don't believe she desired it.

Yet all the same I might have done it.

Her conduct was such that I too became soured— later, indeed, infuriated. Again and again we clashed, and our once quiet home was filled with wrangling and scenes of violence. Quite certainly we were both to blame; but her way of regarding my abominable offence, as she termed it, and the vicious creature who had seduced me—the whole disgraceful, filthy connection—was so repugnant to me that without the least understanding or compassion I condemned her as a vile, despicable creature. I began to loathe her; I gave no thought to the fact that she was my mother and that at one time my feelings for her had been quite different. On the contrary, I believe this even embittered me. Everything about her now seemed to me repulsive, and my tendency to perceive the ludicrous and foolish side of her behaviour and utterances made me as malicious and as evilly observant as herself. I denied myself no opportunity of unmasking her, and I still remember the glee I felt when in her fury she unconsciously revealed that she, who came from humble stock, found it rather gratifying that I did, after all, betray god with a woman of noble birth.

Seeing that she could get nowhere with me, and being at a loss what to do with all her venom, she turned to our old confessor to tell him of me and ask his advice. In reality she cared nothing for his counsel or anyone else's; she was incapable of such a thing, but she knew exactly what she wanted and how to achieve it.

He was deeply distressed by what he heard. But when she asked him to speak to one of my superiors and report me for my offence he flatly refused. He was much attached to me, as I to him, and far too good-hearted a man to act in such a fashion. I had said nothing of the matter at confession, he said, and he would therefore take no cognizance of the sin, however grave it might be.

This seemed to her an outrageous and irresponsible attitude, and so it was. Yet such was his reply.

This old man, whom I greatly revered and loved, spoke with me at length, trying to influence me with wise and gentle words and help me to overcome a passion which as he realised was one that might attack even a spiritual man. I listened to him willingly and submissively, but that was the only way in which I could show the veneration and devotion I felt for him. Gladden him I could not: I was powerless against the passion that ruled me, and I had no choice.

My mother noted his failure and understood that this mild man could never get the better of me or of the evil spirit that had conquered me. She then set herself to exploit his mildness and weakness, and worked upon him ceaselessly to make him speak of me to the priest of St. Thomas's, who bore the chief responsibility for me and my evil-doing. She told him that it was his duty to do so. He eventually admitted the truth of this, though he persisted in his refusal. But in her malice towards me, in her desire to be revenged upon me and to harm me, and not least—as ever—to have her own way—she continued to coerce him and left the poor old man no peace. One may well wonder why she was so fanatical; she seemed possessed, and at length it dawned upon me how violent a nature was hidden beneath her peaceable exterior. Clearly her mother-love—always warped—had twisted into something like hatred for me, and she took no more account of my being her son than I did of her being my mother; in our bitter enmity, at least, we were alike.

At last the old man gave in and accepted the task which she laid upon him as an obligation, but which he had so long and stubbornly refused to undertake.

Later, when he beheld the consequences, he was distraught at what he had done—quite broken by it

—although what he had done was no more than his duty. One should not do one's duty, he repeated over and over again—so I was told—and this incident in his quiet life put years on his age; he is said never to have forgiven himself for it.

So it was this truly good-hearted man—perhaps one of the few good people in a city overflowing with churches and priests and believers and worshippers and religious rabble of all kinds—who in a sense informed against me and was the cause of my downfall. If that is the right term.

Events now moved rapidly, and my fate was soon to be decided.

First, I was suspended from my duties, though secretly for the time being: I was forbidden to tell anyone of it. It would become general knowledge soon enough, I was told, by way of consolation.

Next, an inquiry—secret likewise—was set up to discover what had happened, how my relationship with the woman had begun, which of us had initiated it, and much else. Such questions bordered upon delicate and fateful matters, and Father Benedict—a highly respected, subtle and dangerous man—became involved in the proceedings and was soon largely in control of them.

He visited his penitent and asked her gently whether she had anything on her mind, and whether that was why she had not made her confession to him for so long. If so, he would gladly listen and help her to find peace with her god, for she was very dear to him and he knew what a burden it was to have no one to confide in, and what trouble and distress resulted from it.

He could not have made a more astute or effective appeal, for her heart was indeed heavy on that very account. She was a true believer and therefore unhappy and inwardly torn because of her burden and her grievous rift with god. And although she felt repugnance towards her family confessor, and even feared him, it was a relief to talk of what gave her such anguish, and she fell an easy prey to his life-long experience as a guardian of souls in the circles to which she belonged and in which he was as much at home as herself. He was well-versed in human nature, especially in its vices and infirmities, of which he had a penetrating and possibly even profound understanding, though his judgment was no less incorruptibly strict on that account when need arose. But he was a broadminded man, and did not always consider that such a need existed.

Little by little he drew it all from her.

Thus he learned that she had made her confession to me at St. Thomas's instead of to him, and that our liaison had come about in that way. Hard-pressed —although he addressed her in an unfailingly gentle voice—she admitted that this unlawful attraction had been kindled in the course of confession itself, and that indeed I had exploited this to make advances to her and to pave the way for her seduction. At last I had followed her on her way home from church and gained entry to the palace with her, to achieve my purpose.

Thereafter she had been bound to me by sinful desire, an irresistible passion which she longed to acknowledge in all candour, knowing it to be a mortal sin that condemned her to hell-fire; she must unburden her heart and make full confession. She longed to throw herself into the arms of god and his holy church, sinful and lost as she was: it was, as she now saw, her only course. If there were any atonement, any penance so severe that by it she might be saved from eternal punishment and dragged from the jaws of hell, she would thankfully submit to it. But she could not believe there was.

All this I learned at the interrogation to which I

was summoned before the consistory court, and as a result of which I was deprived of my office, excommunicated, and for ever excluded from the service of the church.

I needn't say how violently I was shattered—not because I was dismissed, thrown out, expelled, but because she had lied about me. About herself and me and our union. Especially was I stricken by her besmirching of that holy night of love that we had experienced together, and which for me was still the greatest miracle that could be. Or was it?

Of course she may not have said all this: they may have exaggerated her accusations against me and her version of what had happened. I could not be sure, for I was completely cut off from any chance of seeing her. All the same . . . In essentials it was true enough, and it more than sufficed to fill me with utter loathing. I left the consistory and my revered superiors and colleagues in a state of violent agitation, fury and contempt.

The man most determined that my sentence should be the sternest was Father Benedict, and it was he who reported what she had said in her confession. His attitude to me was not benevolent, to say the least; indeed I believe that he was offended because instead of turning to him she had confessed to me: an insignificant priest in the insignificant little church of St. Thomas. He was of course quite unaware of the reason for this: she had not mentioned it in her confession. Her true love she had not betrayed: only me.

His sentence upon her was less harsh, one reason no doubt being that she came of good family; moreover, he well knew her peculiarities and her imaginative nature, which had often both diverted and disturbed him, and which he realised might easily lead her astray if she were left to herself or to someone ruthless enough to take advantage of it. In this of course he was aiming at me, and he wholeheartedly shared her own view: that she had been seduced. The fact that throughout the inquiry I uttered not one word in my own defence surprised some people, but served only to confirm them all in their belief that my guilt was fully proven. As indeed it was.

It was through Father Benedict, his confessor of long standing, that the husband learned of her transgression, and no doubt the case was presented to him in the most appropriate way. It must indeed have been a singular topic of conversation for them, the one having so often lent a confidential ear to the other's tales of a long and sinful life, with understanding and indulgence and at times with some measure of enjoyment. It was said that the distinguished old gentleman's bloated, pallid face assumed an amused expression, with a lop-sided smile on his slackened mouth, one corner of which always dribbled. Yet this did not prevent him from locking her up in her room and walling up the damp secret passage which had been discovered to be the means of our transgression. Thus even she did not escape punishment.

Later, it seems, she was allowed to leave her prison, if one may so term it, to go on the pilgrimage that had been laid upon her as atonement for her grievous sin—the pilgrimage that she so ardently desired to make. Or so I heard. By that time I was no longer there.

My dismissal and its cause now became generally known, as had been promised. You may well picture the sensation it aroused in such a city as that, where church and priesthood played so great and central a rôle. A priest and a woman from one of the most eminent and most distinguished families! And a married woman at that! It was something unheard-of, and feeling naturally ran most fiercely against me, as the priestly seducer. The whole of that godly little town leagued itself against me and I became the object of universal disgust and contempt. I could not go out into the street without people hurling invectives after me—the coarsest words that could be thought of—and the children threw stones. Some even spat in my face, or tried to. A colleague of mine at St. Thomas's, of my own age, succeeded, and this appeared to give him great satisfaction. I was hunted and harried as by mad, mangy dogs, persecuted from the moment I showed myself outside, and within by my savage, raging mother. Everywhere! They were after me everywhere.

Man, that evil beast, was in full cry.

At last I could stand it no longer. I left the city— left the house of my mother and the crucified, full of revulsion for it all—and slammed the door after me.

The last I saw of her was her straggling grey locks that stood out from her sunken temples, and her eyes, which were quite wild—almost frightening. What my own eyes looked like I don't know, of course: I couldn't see them. But no doubt she did.

In time I found myself aboard this vessel, where on the whole I have been well content—where life is rough and brutal and bloody, and if not exactly honest, at least not a lie. At sea, the boundless sea, indifferent to all, caring for nothing, neither devil nor god—inhuman. And that is surely good: one *must* feel so if one has learnt to know men. And the prostitutes in the ports—*they* don't pretend to be anything but what they are, and they satisfy me very well with their expert, honest love-making.

Now you have heard my life, and may judge me as you choose.

HE WAS SILENT. Both lay silent in the star-
bright night. No ripple was heard against the hull,
and on all sides the sea lay dark and calm.

Tobias' mind was in a ferment: the only disturbed
thing in all that perfect stillness. The story he had
heard occupied his mind, engrossed him and
troubled him greatly with its bitter message.

Through his melancholy thoughts he heard a short,
quiet laugh from Giovanni: a laugh seemingly without cause. Raising himself on one elbow he found
that Giovanni had done the same, and that he was
feeling for something at his hairy breast. He brought

it out. It was a locket—a plain, smooth locket—no doubt of silver. It looked tiny in his big, calloused hand.

Tobias knew that it must be hers, and when he asked, Giovanni nodded. He had difficulty in opening it with his thick thumbnail, but succeeded after a time, and holding it up in the starlight, which was bright enough to see by, he showed it to Tobias.

It was empty.

He told how he had contrived to steal it from her the last time they were together, when already he guessed that their story was nearing its end. He had not tried to snatch it in a struggle that, as in the beginning, might have ended in a burning embrace, though by then this was hardly likely; he had simply stolen it from her without her noticing, to find out whom she really loved—to rob her at last of her secret.

When he had parted from her for what turned out to be the last time, and was alone again, he opened the locket and found it empty.

Her true love did not exist: he who was unlike the rest of us, he with the pure brow, he of whom she was to testify before god. He did not exist— had never existed.

She was said to have been distracted when she discovered her loss—utterly broken by it. Probably she never knew how it had disappeared and supposed that she had dropped it.

But the portrait of the beloved was gone for ever.

For a while they lay silent again, side by side, not looking at each other.

"What happened to her afterwards?" Tobias asked in a low voice. "Do you know? Is she still alive?"

"No, she died long, long ago. She died on the pilgrimage I spoke of."

"I see. And what pilgrimage was that? To what place?"

"It was a pilgrimage to the Holy Land."

"Oh . . . Was it?"

"Yes. But she never arrived. She died just as they sighted land, from what I heard."

"So she didn't get there. Not even that . . ."

"No."

Tobias clasped his hands over his chest and looked up into the burning sky of stars.

She never arrived—never arrived.

He thought about the highest and holiest in life

and of what nature it might be: that perhaps it exists only as a dream and cannot survive reality, the awakening. But that it does nevertheless exist. That perfect love exists and the Holy Land exists; it is just that we cannot reach it. That perhaps we are only on our way there—only pilgrims at sea.

Yet the sea is not everything: it cannot be. There must be something beyond it, there must be a land beyond the great desolate expanses and the great deeps which are indifferent to all things: a land we cannot reach but to which nevertheless we are on our way.

And he thought of how Giovanni had kept that locket, cherished it and never wanted to part with it, but had worn it constantly at his breast, although it was empty. And even had it not been empty, it would have contained the likeness of another man. Yet he had always worn it, as she too had worn it at her breast, close to her heart.

How precious, how indispensable a thing it must be.

Although it was empty.

Thus he lay thinking, with his hands clasped upon his chest and his eyes on the shining stars, while the ship glided imperceptibly forward over the endless sea, without a goal.

In 1940 Pär Lagerkvist was elected one of the eighteen "immortals" of the Swedish Academy. Within a decade this honor gained international luster when he received the Nobel Prize. But Lagerkvist's career as playwright, novelist, poet and thinker has been an evolution rather than an outburst, and covers half a century of nearly forty books.

Even in his earliest works Lagerkvist showed a leaning toward experimentation and a spirit of opposition. After a visit to Paris in 1913, he returned to Stockholm imbued with the many new trends he had discovered in the art world there, especially cubism and expressionism, and quickly published a much-debated pamphlet. This work had two significant subtitles: "The decadence of modern fiction—the vitality of modern art." In this booklet he upheld the virility and originality of cubism, and wanted to see the same force and power permeate literature. He turned against naturalistic writing, called for a more sober and severe artistry, and held up as models the native tales and folklore of many countries and eras, among them the ancient Icelandic sagas, the Koran, and the Bible.

With the passage of time he developed a simpler, more concentrated style. But always humanitarian in aim, he has continued to pursue mankind's struggles for good and evil.

Though he has spent long periods in other European countries, Lagerkvist makes his home in his native Sweden.